Labyrinth

By Melanie Joyce
Illustrated by
Anthony Williams

Titles in Full Flight 7

Midsummer Mutants	David Orme
Beek...	...rson
Laby...	...oyce
The I...	...es
Sci-Fi...	...n
Ghos...	...ll
Stone...	...ylor
Alien...	...er
Jet Pa...	...er
Hero: A War Dog's Tale	Jane A C West

Badger Publishing Limited
Suite G08, Business & Technology Centre
Bessemer Drive, Stevenage, Hertfordshire SG1 2DX
Telephone: 01438 791037   Fax: 01438 791036
www.badger-publishing.co.uk

Labyrinth ISBN 978-1-84926-255-2

Labyrinth © Melanie Joyce 2010
Complete work © Badger Publishing Limited 2010

Badger Publishing would like to thank Jonny Zucker for his help in putting this series together.

Publisher: David Jamieson
Editor: Danny Pearson
Design: Fiona Grant
Illustration: Anthony Williams
Printed and bound in China through Colorcraft Ltd., Hong Kong

Labyrinth

Contents

Badger Publishing

New words:

game	dragged
tunnel	rumbled
player	creature
weather	electricity
crashed	breathing

Main characters:

Lexie

John

Chapter 1

Beginnings

The game was about to begin.

Lexie and John waited. A sliding door opened.

It led into a room. They walked in.

There were two chairs. There were two computers.

Lexie and John sat down. They put on headsets.

"Welcome to Labyrinth," said a voice. "A game of virtual reality. Prize money today is £20,000."

"The labyrinth is a maze of tunnels. Players must reach the centre. They must key in a kill code. This will stop the virtual reality. Today's code is 6996005."

"Sounds easy," said John.

The voice spoke again.
"The labyrinth has many secrets. There are dead ends. There are traps. Players beware."

"I can't wait!" said John.

"Attach game probes," continued the voice.

The probes moved into position.

A clap of thunder came from outside.

It made Lexie jump.
"Nothing virtual about that," she said.

"The weather's gone crazy, lately."
She felt uneasy.

Was it pre-game nerves?

"Ten seconds to entry," said the voice.
"10...9...8...7...6..."

The probes began to pulse.

"Ready?" said Lexie.

"Ready," replied John.

They closed their eyes.
"5...4...3...2...1."

It was time to enter Labyrinth.

Chapter 2
The Storm

Outside, the storm struck suddenly.

A thunderbolt split the air. It tore downwards.

It hit the Labyrinth control room.

There was an explosion. The computers crashed. The head controller shouted. "Switch on the back-up power!"

The emergency power came on.

The computers came back to life.
However, there was something wrong.

"The energy levels are in overload.
The labyrinth is changing.
It's creating an earthquake!"

"Stop the game!" shouted the head
controller. "Get them out of there."

It was too late.

Lexie and John opened their eyes.

They were underground. They were in a tunnel.

It was dimly lit. In the distance there was a rumble.

They crept forward.

The tunnel shook slightly.

"What was that?" said Lexie. She felt scared.

John laughed. "It's virtual reality, Lexie. It's not real."

The rumbling came closer. The tunnel shook again.

Lexie and John were thrown to the floor.

The lights went out. It was pitch black.

Chapter 3

Underworld

The shaking stopped.

Lexie reached for her torch.

"Ouch!" she complained.
Her bruised arm hurt.

John was worried.
"We aren't supposed to get hurt.
Something's wrong."

He tapped his headset. There was
only noisy static.

Something moved in the dark.
It touched Lexie.

She jumped up quickly. She shone the
torch. There was nothing there.

"This place is creepy," she said.
"I don't like it."

The tunnel lights went on and off.

John tapped the headset again.
"Can anyone hear me?"

The static cleared. The lights came on.
A voice spoke. It sounded urgent.
"The mainframe is damaged. We are
trying to repair it. There is something
you must know..."

A huge tremor shook the tunnel.

The lights faded. The static returned.
John could hardly hear the voice.

"...labyrinth changing... central
chamber...danger..."

There was a huge shudder. The signal
went dead.

Chapter 4

It Breathes

Something moved again.

Lexie spun round. The tunnel wall
moved. She touched it.

Fear gripped her. She could see it in John's face too.

"We've got to find the centre. Let's go. Hurry."

The tunnels grew darker. They twisted like snakes.

"It's like we're being watched," said Lexie.

"We are," whispered John. "Look up."

The creature was on the ceiling. It grew out of the skin.

They aimed their lasers. The lasers jammed.

"Run!"

They ran down the tunnel. They came to a dead end. There was a door.

Lexie ran towards the door.
"It might be a way out!"

The door opened.

"No!" screamed John. "It's a trap!"

He dived towards Lexie. John fell near the door.

Something grabbed him. It dragged him back.

"Help!"

John was pulled like a ragdoll. He was pulled through the doorway. The door slammed shut.

Lexie was alone.

She was alone in the labyrinth.

It was the enemy. It had taken John. Was she next?

She had to get to the centre. It was her only chance.

Chapter 5

Game Over

The tunnels grew hotter. They grew darker.

Would they ever end?

Suddenly there was a light.

Lexie stepped into a chamber. It buzzed with electricity. She was at the centre.

She could see the keypad. She stepped forward.

A bolt of energy hit her. Lexie fell to the floor.

John lay in the dark.

His leg ached. Was it broken?

A voice came over the headset.
The signal was weak. "Re-connect...
Lexie...code..."

John had to help Lexie. He shook his
wrist laser. He aimed it at the door.

It blasted open.

In the chamber, Lexie moved. She felt weak.

"I have to key in the code."
She reached upwards.
6996...

The walls of the chamber moved. They were like giant lungs. The labyrinth breathed. It wanted to stop Lexie.

The terrible force struck again. Lexie collapsed.

Someone called to her.

"Lexie - the code."

It was John. He was injured. He raised his wrist laser. The force turned on him.

"I can't hold it for long. Hurry, Lexie!"

Lexie stretched up.

Her hand shook. The force raged.

The sound was terrible. Bolts of electricity split the air.

The labyrinth was going to destroy them.

There was nothing to lose. Lexie pressed the numbers.

6996005.

There was dead silence.

"Game over," said the computer.

The chamber disappeared.

All that remained was a metal box.

Lexie and John opened the box.
Inside was
£20,000.

They began to laugh.

"We won the prize money!"

The nightmare was over.

Outside, the storm had cleared.

Lexie and John looked up at the Sun.
They looked at the blue sky.

"I prefer the real world," said Lexie.

"It's a lot safer than the Labyrinth."

Earthquakes

- *The Earth's surface is like a giant jigsaw puzzle.*

- *The pieces of the puzzle are called tectonic plates.*

- *The plates move around. Sometimes they slide past one another.*

- *The place where they slide is called a fault. When the plates touch, they create a powerful energy.*

- *The energy ripples through the Earth. The ripples are called seismic waves. They make the ground shake.*

- *This is called an earthquake.*

- *The energy released by an earthquake is measured on a scale between 1 and 9. This is known as the Richter scale.*

- *An earthquake of 1 would not be felt on the surface. An earthquake of 9 would be incredibly destructive.*

- *The largest ever-recorded earthquake was in Chile in 1960. It measured about 9.2 on the Richter scale.*

- *Scientists cannot predict earthquakes. They know where they might happen. However, they cannot say when.*

Questions

- What game do John and Lexie play?

- How much is the prize money?

- What numbers make up the kill code?

- Who is pulled through the doorway?

- What hits the control room?

- What do the tunnel walls feel like?